Hilda glared at Salem. "Now you've really done it."

Salem hung his head. "I don't know what came over me!" His nose itched and he sneezed. "I didn't mean to be bad. I just didn't want my shots!"

Hilda and Zelda both backed away from the table. They looked really sad.

"What?" Salem sneezed three times.

"I told you you'd be very sorry if you didn't cooperate, Salem," Zelda said.

"There's nothing we can do to help you now." Hilda shook her head.

"About what?" Salem started sneezing and he couldn't stop.

Sabrina, the Teenage Witch™
Salem's Tails™

Available from MINSTREL Books

Sabrina
The Teenage Witch®

Salem's Tails®

WORTH A SHOT

Diana G. Gallagher

Based upon the characters in Archie Comics

And based upon the television series
Sabrina, The Teenage Witch
Created for television by Nell Scovell
Developed for television by Jonathan Schmock

Illustrated by Mark Dubowski

A MINSTREL®
BOOK

Published by POCKET BOOKS
New York   London   Toronto   Sydney   Singapore

This book is a work of fiction. Names, characters, places and incidents are products of the author's imagination or are used fictitiously. Any resemblance to actual events or locales or persons living or dead is entirely coincidental.

A MINSTREL PAPERBACK *Original*

 A Minstrel Book published by
POCKET BOOKS, a division of Simon & Schuster Inc.
1230 Avenue of the Americas, New York, NY 10020

Salem Quotes taken from the episode "Boy, Was My Face Red" Written by Carrie Honigblum & Renee Phillips

ISBN: 0-671-03834-6

First Minstrel Books printing March 2000

10 9 8 7 6 5 4 3 2 1

A MINSTREL BOOK and colophon are registered trademarks of Simon & Schuster Inc.

SABRINA THE TEENAGE WITCH and all related titles, logos and characters are trademarks of Archie Comics Publications, Inc.

Cover photo by Pat Hill Studio

Printed in the U.S.A.

For my grandson,
John Alan Streb, Jr.
With all my love.

"Not the vet! Cold hands, cold table, and the probing. Oh, the probing!"

—*Salem*

WORTH A SHOT

Chapter 1

Salem woke up instantly. He wasn't sure if he had *really* heard Hilda say "shrimp snack."

"Maybe it was just a dream." The cat sat up on Sabrina's bed and cocked his head. Cabinet doors banged open and closed in the kitchen. Hilda had gone to the grocery store while he was taking his afternoon nap!

"Shrimp snack!" Sabrina exclaimed

loudly. "Is it Salem's birthday, Aunt Hilda?"

"No," Hilda said. "I just felt like doing something special for him."

Yes! Salem jumped to the floor and dashed down the upstairs hall. It wasn't a dream! Hilda had dried shrimp bits for him in the kitchen.

"Be careful or you'll spoil him, Hilda," Zelda said. "Shrimp is one of Salem's favorite foods."

Ranking second only to caviar, Salem thought as he bounded down the stairs. *And maybe tuna.*

"Are you going to give the shrimp snacks to Salem now?" Sabrina asked. "Or wait until later?"

Now! Now! Salem raced toward the dining room.

"Why make him wait?" Hilda paused,

then shouted. "Salem! You've got shrimp! Come and get it!"

Salem skidded to a halt under the dining room table. Something suddenly smelled fishy and it wasn't shrimp snacks.

The cat stared at the closed door into the kitchen. Hilda and Zelda were always worried about his weight. And he was always on some awful diet.

So why does Hilda want to stuff me with shrimp snacks? Salem wondered. *There has to be a catch.*

A bath? Salem hated getting wet.

Or some new flea treatment that will make me smell like roses?

The phone rang.

"Hello?" Hilda answered. "Yes, Dr. Adams. No, I haven't forgotten our appointment. We'll be there by four."

"Who's Dr. Adams?" Sabrina asked.

3

"The new vet." Zelda sighed. "Salem loved Dr. Werner, but we couldn't go back after she heard him talk."

Vet! Salem gasped. He wasn't sick, so an appointment could only mean one thing. *Shots!*

"If I don't get to Dr. Adams's office by four, the doctor won't be able to see Salem today," Hilda said. "And he's a month overdue for his shots."

I knew it! Salem shuddered.

"Where is Salem?" Sabrina opened the dining room door. "He loves shrimp snacks."

Time to play the invisible cat. Salem flattened himself on the carpet and froze. His heart pounded as Sabrina scanned the room. He began to breathe again when she shrugged and closed the door.

"I thought he'd come running when he knew we had shrimp snacks." Hilda sounded annoyed.

Salem *had* almost run right into Hilda's trap. He loved shrimp snacks, but he hated getting shots more.

"It's already three-thirty!" Zelda exclaimed. "If we don't find him in fifteen minutes, you'll have to cancel his appointment."

Cancel my vet appointment! Now, wouldn't that *be a shame?*

Salem chuckled softly as he padded back toward the stairs. He knew a dozen places to hide where no one could find him. Staying out of sight for fifteen minutes would be easy.

"He might be asleep in my room," Sabrina said. "I'll go look."

Salem raced up the stairs.

"Search the whole second floor, Sabrina," Hilda called out. "I'll take the downstairs, and you look outside, Zelda. He's got to be here somewhere."

Salem trotted down the hall to Hilda's room. He ducked through the door just as Sabrina reached the landing. She stopped to look in the wicker basket by the linen closet. He hid in there sometimes, but not *this* time!

"Salem?" Sabrina walked into her room.

"What?" Salem whispered as he slipped into Hilda's closet. It was jam-packed with weird things she had collected. Zelda made Hilda store most of her strange stuff in the dungeon. But Hilda kept her extra-special things in the large walk-in closet.

"Salem! Where are you?" Sabrina shouted from the hall.

It was dark in the closet, but Salem could see in the dark. That was one good thing about being a cat.

Salem squeezed between a football helmet and a ship's anchor. Then he ducked behind a pair of snowshoes. Hilda's tuba was lying on its side in a corner.

"They'll never find me here." Salem crawled inside the huge horn. Hilda had bought the tuba at a garage sale, but she never played it.

"Come on, Salem!" Sabrina came into Hilda's room. She looked under the bed and then under the dresser. "Come out, come out, wherever you are."

Not a chance! Salem stayed totally still when Sabrina looked in the closet. He held his breath when she stepped inside and turned on the light.

"I know you're in here, Salem." Sab-

7

rina moved a pair of cowboy boots and a ballerina tutu.

She doesn't know, Salem told himself. *She's just guessing.* Still, he got nervous when Sabrina pushed the football helmet aside. She was getting too close!

"Any luck?" Zelda walked in.

"No." Sabrina threw up her hands and left the closet. "We're not gonna find Salem if he doesn't want to be found. He's probably watching us and laughing."

Yep! Salem grinned.

"Probably." Zelda sighed. "But he won't have the last laugh."

"What do you mean?" Sabrina asked.

"I'm going to make another vet appointment for tomorrow," Zelda said. "If Salem doesn't cooperate and get his shots, he'll be very, very sorry."

No, I won't, Salem thought. *I hate getting shots!*

"Is this another one of those witch rules you can't talk about, Aunt Zelda?" Sabrina followed Zelda out of the room.

"Only if you're a familiar like Salem." Zelda's voice faded as she headed back down the hall.

Salem decided to stay in the tuba for another ten minutes. Just to be sure. And he wasn't worried about some old witch rule. The Witches' Council had already turned him into a cat for trying to take over the world.

"What could be worse than that?"

Salem knew one thing for sure. Since he *was* a cat, *nothing* could be as bad as getting shots!

9

Chapter 2

Salem was starving! His stomach rumbled as he peeked out from under the sofa.

He had almost walked into another trap when he left Hilda's closet yesterday afternoon. Hilda and Zelda knew he would be hungry. They had waited in the kitchen to capture him when he showed up for dinner.

But he had seen the cat carrier by the back door.

And he had disappeared again—fast!

It was five o'clock in the morning now. Everyone was still asleep.

Salem crept out from under the sofa. His muscles were stiff from lying flat for so long. He stretched. He was so hungry even low-fat dry cat food would taste good.

"But Hilda and Zelda have probably set another trap." Salem's stomach growled.

Salem took a step toward the kitchen, then stopped. He just *knew* he was going to get caught. And *that* meant getting his shots!

"I have to make sure Hilda and Zelda can't take me to the vet's. But how?"

Salem suddenly had a great idea. Hilda and Zelda always drove the car when they had an appointment with a mortal.

"But they can't drive the car if they don't have the keys!"

11

Salem looked over his shoulder. Hilda's handbag was on the piano. He padded over and fished her car keys out with his teeth.

Next Salem went to the closet in the foyer. He got Zelda's keys out of her coat pocket. He got the spare keys from Zelda's desk, too. Then he sat down by the pile.

Salem's tail twitched. He had to hide the keys so a search-and-locate spell couldn't find them. Some place where they would be in plain sight but *not* in plain sight.

"The junk drawer!"

Salem giggled as he carried Hilda's keys into the kitchen. He jumped onto the counter and opened the junk drawer with his paw.

Perfect! Every key to every car Hilda

and Zelda had ever owned was in the drawer. He dropped Hilda's keys into the pile of old keys.

Salem looked at his food dish on the middle counter. It was full of King Kitty Tuna Supreme. His stomach gurgled and his mouth watered. He was so hungry!

"But first things first." Salem got the other two sets of keys. After he put them in the junk drawer, he leaped toward his bowl on the middle counter.

"Food!" Salem landed by his food dish. *Click*.

A gigantic cat carrier suddenly appeared around Salem and the bowl. It covered the whole counter. It even had a kitty litter box and a water bowl.

"Those sneaky witches!" Salem huffed. Hilda and Zelda had put a *spell* on the counter.

13

Salem wasn't worried, though. After he stuffed himself with Tuna Supreme, he'd curl up and sleep. Hilda and Zelda wouldn't know their car keys were missing until it was time to leave for the vet's.

By the time they found the keys, it would be too late to make his appointment—again.

"Everything is under control."

"Okay, Salem." Hilda glared at the black cat. "Where are they?"

"What?" Salem pressed his nose against the wire cage door.

"You know what, Salem." Zelda rolled her eyes. "The car keys!"

"Are they missing?" Salem asked innocently.

Hilda and Zelda exchanged annoyed glances.

"Yes, they are." Hilda scowled. "We can't even find the spare set."

"But hiding our keys so we can't drive you to the vet isn't going to work." Zelda shook her finger at Salem. "I can find them with a search-and-locate spell."

"And we've got plenty of time before your appointment." Hilda patted the top of the cage. "You *are* getting your shots today, Salem."

We'll just see about that! Salem sat down when Zelda closed her eyes. He crossed his front paws for luck as she cast a search-and-locate spell.

Zelda raised her finger.

*"Come out, come out wherever you are,
    All the keys to Spellman cars."*

Zelda pointed. "That should do it."

15

Hilda folded her arms and glanced around the kitchen.

Salem tensed as the junk drawer popped open and dumped *all* the keys on the floor.

Zelda frowned. "Those are all our *old* car keys!"

Yes! Salem didn't dare laugh out loud. The keys to Hilda's car were in the pile with the old car keys.

But Hilda and Zelda didn't look closely. They thought the spell had goofed.

"You must have done something wrong, Zelda," Hilda said. "Let me try." She squeezed her eyes shut.

"Search and locate, if you please,
All the Spellman's missing keys."

Hilda pointed. Two seconds later

dozens of strange things appeared in the kitchen.

Zelda jumped when a big square stone landed on the table. "Oh, my. I wondered what happened to that."

"What?" Salem asked. "That rock?"

"It's a keystone. It was supposed to be part of a stone archway." Zelda shrugged. "In a castle we built three hundred years ago."

"Except we couldn't find it." Hilda shook her head. "So we had a stone archway with a big hole on top."

"Well, that's one key that isn't missing anymore," Salem said. He couldn't believe how well his plan was working!

"And here are some others!" Zelda picked up a handful of small, round buttons. They had letters printed on them. "Here's the A, H, C, and Y keys that fell

off my typewriter when I moved in 1942."

Salem cocked his head when he heard a steady noise. It sounded like a violin that was stuck on one note. "What key is that?"

"The key of F!" Hilda clasped her hands. "I never could find the key of F on my very first violin!"

Zelda pointed to a pile of small white rectangles. "Aren't those the keys that fell off the piano we had back in 1893?"

"Probably." Hilda exhaled loudly. "We've found every key we've ever lost—except the car keys!"

"What a pity." Salem sighed. "Guess you'll just have to cancel my appointment."

"Not a chance!" Hilda's eyes flashed.

"We're running out of vets in Westbridge. We don't dare cancel again."

"We don't have to cancel," Zelda said. "Witches don't need keys to start the car. We can use magic."

Salem started to panic. "But it's already too late to make my appointment on time!"

"It's too late if we drive." Hilda grinned. "Just because we don't *like* to pop into mortal offices doesn't mean we *can't*."

Salem's fur stood up on his back. "Isn't that against the witch rules or something?"

"Nope!" Hilda pointed at the large carrier cage. It shrank back down to normal size. The kitty litter box and bowls were outside the cage, but Salem was still trapped inside.

"Can't we discuss this?" Salem pleaded.

"Nope!" Zelda picked up the carrier and snapped her fingers.

"Nooooo!" Salem wailed as they popped into the hallway outside Dr. Adams's clinic. "I hate shots!"

Chapter 3

Hilda started to open the door into the vet's office.

Salem tensed. "Wait!"

"What?" Hilda eyed him narrowly. "You're getting your shots. No arguments."

"I know! But at least let me go to my doom with dignity." Salem rattled the wire cage door. "Let me out of here!"

Zelda frowned. "Only if you prom-

ise on your cat's honor not to run away."

"Or talk!" Hilda added.

Salem held up his paw. "I promise on my cat's honor not to run away or talk."

"Okay, then." Zelda opened the cage. After Salem stepped out, she pointed and the carrier disappeared. "I know you won't break your cat's oath."

"No way!" Salem gasped. "I won't risk being a cat for *another* hundred years."

"Or worse." Hilda opened the office door.

"Don't remind me." Salem licked his paw and smoothed his whiskers. "I have nightmares about that poor cat who was turned into a mouse. No, thank you!"

"Be brave, Salem." Zelda stepped back to let Salem go inside ahead of her. "It'll be over pretty soon."

"Easy for you to say." Salem sobbed. "You're not getting your shots!"

Salem couldn't think of a way to escape. So he lifted his chin and marched through the door. He didn't want to look like a sissy in front of the other pets.

Hilda went up to the counter to check in. Zelda sat in a chair near an elderly lady. She had a small dog on her lap.

Aha! Salem looked at the black-and-white dog. It had big, round eyes, a flat muzzle and long hair. *That dog looks like a mop that ran into a wall!*

The little dog jumped up when it saw Salem. "Arf! Arf, arf, arf!"

"Shhhh, Tiger!" The elderly lady shook her finger at the dog.

"Grrrrr." Tiger growled, but he stopped barking.

23

Salem jumped up on the chair between Zelda and the older woman. He stared at Tiger.

The dog's top lip was caught under one of its front fangs. It looked like it was sneering!

Don't mess with me, dog, Salem thought. *I'm a cat who's having a very bad day.*

Tiger snorted and looked away. He curled up on the lady's lap.

I win! Salem glanced at Zelda. She was reading a magazine. Hilda was still standing at the counter.

Cool! I can have some more fun. Salem batted the dog's tail and quickly pulled his paw back. *I am* so *bad.*

Tiger jumped up and whirled to face the cat. "Arf! Arf, arf, arf!"

Salem stared at the ceiling.

"Bad dog, Tiger!" The lady tugged his leash. "Lie down and be quiet."

"Arf!" Tiger glared at the cat. Then he lay down again.

Zelda lowered her magazine and frowned. "Are you behaving yourself, Salem?"

Who me? Salem opened his eyes wide and nodded. As soon as she looked away, he batted the dog again.

"Arf!" Tiger jumped up so fast he slipped off the lady's lap. He landed on the floor with a loud *thud*. The dog shook its head. He seemed surprised to find that he was on the floor.

Oops! Sorry about that! Salem chuckled under his breath.

"Tiger!" The elderly lady leaned over. "Are you all right?"

25

Hilda walked up. She glared at Salem and whispered loudly. "I saw that!"

What? Salem blinked. Sometimes he was glad he couldn't talk around mortals. Hilda would forget what he had done by the time they left the vet's office. Then he wouldn't have to explain.

The vet's assistant came into the waiting room. "It's Tiger's turn."

The lady picked up Tiger and headed toward the exam rooms.

Salem sighed. He wasn't that fond of dogs, but he hoped Tiger didn't have to get shots. Not even dogs deserved that!

Shots! Salem moaned. *Now I'm going to think about getting shots. And that just makes it worse!*

Hilda sat down beside Zelda. "Salem's next."

Oh, no! Salem flopped on his stomach

and covered his face with his paws. If he couldn't *see* what was happening, maybe it wouldn't happen.

The office door opened. Salem tried to keep his eyes closed, but he was too curious. He was a cat, after all. He opened one eye.

A thin man sat down in the chair beside him. The man had a small green-and-yellow parrot on his shoulder.

Oh, boy! It's a bird! Salem sat up. He loved to chase birds, even though he never caught one. It was very frustrating. He couldn't chase this bird. *But I can give it a nifty scare.*

Salem narrowed his eyes and stared.

"Awwwk!" The parrot looked at the cat and cocked its head. It was curious, not frightened.

What? Salem bristled. *Haven't you ever seen a cat, you stupid bird?*

The bird walked along the man's shoulder, moving closer to Salem. It stopped, cocked its head, and whistled.

You are *a stupid bird!* Salem was amazed. The parrot was only a few inches from his face. *Other cats have guys like you for lunch!*

The bird moved to the edge of the man's shoulder and stretched toward Salem.

Salem stared into the parrot's beady, little eyes. He wouldn't ever hurt a bird, but the bird didn't know that. He couldn't believe it wasn't afraid of him. *I'm a cat! With an attitude!*

"Awk!" The bird's head jerked forward, and he pecked Salem's nose.

"Yeow!" Salem jumped back. *That hurt!*

The parrot whistled and moved back to lean against the man's neck.

The man chirped at the bird. "It's okay, Sunshine. You're just getting your wings clipped."

How about getting his beak dulled! Salem rubbed his sore nose. *What an insult! I've been bitten by a bird!*

"Bird, bird, bird!" the parrot squawked. "I'm a bird. Awk, awk, awk!"

And now it's laughing at me! Salem was furious. He had to show the little, feathered bully that he wasn't afraid. His cat-esteem demanded it! He started to hiss.

The assistant called his name. "Salem Saberhagen."

"Come on, Salem." Zelda stood up and dropped her magazine.

No! Not yet! Salem instantly forgot about the parrot. He started to shake. *Take someone else first! Take everyone else first!*

29

"We can't keep Dr. Adams waiting." Hilda picked Salem up.

Salem buried his head under her arm and shut his eyes.

Maybe this is all a bad dream! Maybe I'm really asleep in Sabrina's room.

Salem's paws touched hard, cold steel. *That's not Sabrina's bed!*

Salem's eyes snapped open. He was sitting on a high examining table. The vet's shot supplies were on a smaller table to the side.

Uh-uh. No way. Not *gonna happen!*

"Hello, ladies." The vet grunted as he walked in. He was short with a bald spot on top of his head. His glasses rested on the tip of his nose, and his big teeth gleamed when he smiled. "I'm glad you finally made it."

"We had car trouble yesterday," Hilda explained.

"Thank you for giving us another appointment today, Dr. Adams." Zelda smiled.

Salem's fur stood on end as the vet turned to him.

"And this must be my new patient." Dr. Adams reached out to pet Salem's head. "Hi, Salem."

Salem shrank back and hissed. *Take a look at those fangs, Doc!*

Then Salem put out his claws. He was very careful not to hit the vet's hand when he batted the air. But the pretend attack worked!

"Oh, dear!" Dr. Adams jumped back like he had been scratched, even though Salem hadn't touched him.

"Salem!" Hilda snapped. "No!"

The vet stumbled into a chair and lost his balance. He hit his head on the wall when he fell.

Zelda gasped. "I'm so sorry, Doctor!"

I'm not! Salem hissed again. Just in case the vet hadn't gotten the message.

"We all have bad days." Dr. Adams stood up and rubbed his balding head. "Maybe we should try again next week. When he's calmer. Goodbye!" He left.

Hilda glared at Salem, "Now, you've really done it."

Salem hung his head. "I don't know what came over me!" His nose itched and he sneezed. "I didn't mean to be bad. I just didn't want my shots!"

Hilda and Zelda both backed away from the table. They looked really sad.

"What?" Salem sneezed three times.

32

"I told you you'd be very sorry if you didn't cooperate, Salem," Zelda said.

"There's nothing we can do to help you now." Hilda shook her head.

"About what?" Salem started sneezing and he couldn't stop.

Chapter 4

Salem ran upstairs the instant Hilda and Zelda popped him home.

He was really scared now!

"I don't know what I did. Or why it was so terrible." Salem hadn't given Hilda and Zelda a chance to explain.

"But I'm in *big* trouble!" Salem scratched his itchy nose. "Achoooo!"

Salem had lived with Hilda and Zelda for thirty years. Ever since the Witches'

Council had turned him into a cat. He knew that Sabrina's aunts were really good witches.

If Hilda and Zelda couldn't help him, no one could.

"Or maybe they just *won't* help!"

Salem dashed into Sabrina's bedroom and scooted under her bed. He curled up by the wall. At least the sneezing had stopped.

Salem slept until he heard Sabrina come home from school.

"Hello!" Sabrina called out and slammed the front door. "Anybody home?"

"In the kitchen!" Hilda shouted.

"Sabrina!" Salem exclaimed. "Maybe *she'll* help me."

Salem crept out from under the bed and paused. First he had to find out why he needed help!

"Besides, I haven't eaten since I had breakfast in a giant cat carrier!"

Salem padded to the top of the stairs and looked down. If his crime was so awful, maybe the Other Realm Police were down there! *Just waiting to nab me!*

His stomach rumbled.

"Naw!" Salem trotted down the stairs. The Other Realm Police didn't wait for anyone. They just burst in from the linen closet. Like when Sabrina had become like Libby and had tried to take over the world!

Salem's nose tingled as he darted through the living room. He sneezed on his way through the dining room. His eyes started to water when he padded through the kitchen door.

"Achoo! Achoo!"

Hilda, Zelda, and Sabrina were sitting

at the kitchen table. They were drinking tea and eating cookies. They all turned to stare at him.

"Goodness, Salem!" Sabrina frowned. "Your eyes are all red. Are you sick?"

"Ahm all stuffed up! Achoo!" Salem dragged himself to the counter. Now his skin was beginning to itch! "I'm too weak to jump up."

Zelda picked him up and set him on the counter. He started sneezing and couldn't stop!

"Sorry, Salem!" Zelda quickly sat back down.

"You should be!" Salem sniffled, then sneezed four times. "I must have caught a cat cold at the vet's office!"

"Well, not exactly," Hilda said.

"Although your problem does have

37

something to do with the vet." Zelda shrugged.

"What problem?" Sabrina asked.

"That's what I want to know. Achoo!" Salem rubbed his eyes with his paw. His face fur was all wet. *Yuck!*

"Well, Salem, there are rules for warlocks who have been turned into cats," Zelda said.

Sabrina rolled her eyes. "Rules are a pain!"

"Yes, but we all have to follow them." Hilda sipped her tea. "And Salem has to do all the things regular cats do."

"Like get his regular cat shots." Zelda looked at Salem. "And you didn't cooperate."

"Is it *my* fault the vet couldn't deal with a hissing cat?" Salem tried not to sneeze. He sneezed anyway.

"We told you that you'd be sorry." Hilda heaved a sad sigh. "And I'm sorry you didn't listen."

"But what does *that* have to do with all the sneezing?" Sabrina winced when Salem sneezed again.

"Yeah!" Salem was sure he wouldn't like the answer. But he had to know. "Do I have no-shot flu or something?"

"Much worse, I'm afraid," Hilda said.

"Depending on how you feel about us," Zelda added.

Salem blinked. "Huh?"

Hilda slowly set down her cup. "You wouldn't get your shots, so now you're allergic to Spellmans."

"What!" Sabrina exclaimed.

Salem sat back. "Cats can't be allergic to people. People are allergic to cats! Like my mother!"

"You're not allergic to *all* people, Salem." Zelda picked up a cookie. "Just Spellmans."

"You mean us?" Sabrina's eyes widened. "Oh, no!"

"But, but—" Salem was stunned. He sneezed. "I can't live another seventy years sneezing and itching like crazy!"

"You don't have to." Hilda poured more tea. "You've got two choices."

Sabrina sagged. "That's a relief."

Salem wasn't relieved yet. There had to be a catch. There was always a catch. "What choices?"

Zelda held up a finger. "Number one. If you get an allergy shot every day, you can stay with us."

Salem gasped. "A shot *every* day!"

Hilda nodded. "So you won't sneeze and itch."

I don't think so! Salem collapsed onto his stomach. Getting a shot every day was the worst thing he could imagine.

"What's my second choice?"

"You can go live with someone else," Zelda said. "Who isn't a Spellman."

Salem sneezed. When he finished, he had already made his decision. "Well, that's a no-brainer."

Sabrina grinned. "You'd do anything to stay with us, right, Salem?"

"Anything but shots." Salem took a deep breath. "So I guess I'll have to live with someone else."

Sabrina, Hilda, and Zelda just stared at him.

"After dinner," Salem said.

Chapter 5

The next morning Salem sat on the front porch. All his favorite toys were in a pile at his feet. Hilda and Zelda stood by the front door. It was time to leave.

Sabrina came outside with a bag of Salem's favorite cat treats. She put the bag with his toys. "I thought you might need these, Salem. Your new owner won't know what you like."

"No problem," Salem said. "Achoo! I'll tell them as soon as I arrive. Achoo."

"You can't talk!" Hilda leaned over. "You won't be living with a witch, Salem."

Zelda nodded. "Your new owner will be a mortal."

"What?" Salem stood up. How could he train his new owner properly if he couldn't talk? "Achoo! You didn't tell me that part!"

Hilda shrugged. "Would it make a difference?"

Salem sighed. "Probably not."

"There's still time to change your mind, Salem." Sabrina looked at him hopefully.

Salem sadly shook his head. He didn't want to leave the Spellmans. He would really miss them. But he hated shots too much to stay.

"Well, goodbye, Salem." Hilda smiled. "It's been fun."

"While it lasted." Zelda raised her finger.

"Wait! Achoo!" Salem tensed. "Where are you sending me? Is my new owner nice?"

Zelda shrugged. "I don't know, Salem. The New Homes for Bad Cats people decide where to send you. I just point."

"But what if I don't like it?" Salem wailed.

"Then just ask to go someplace else and the Bad Cats people will send you," Zelda said. "But you can only try three new homes. Then you're stuck."

"It's time to go, Salem." Hilda waved.

"But—" Salem sneezed.

Zelda pointed.

In the blink of an eye Salem was standing on another front porch. This porch was green with white trim.

"Hey! What happened to my toys and treats?" Salem looked around, but his things weren't there. "Rats!"

"Oh, look, Mommy!" A young girl with curly red hair looked through the screen door. "A kitty!"

"Isn't that wonderful, Katy!" A tall woman stood behind the girl. She smiled. "Just what you wanted for your sixth birthday tomorrow!"

Salem perked up. Katy and her mother were glad to see him! That was good.

"Oh, wow!" Katy clapped her hands. Then she ran out and picked Salem up. She gave him a huge hug.

Salem grunted. *Not so hard, Katy! I can't breathe!*

"I bet he's hungry," Katy said.

45

Smart kid! I'm always hungry! Salem purred and rubbed his face against Katy's cheek. *Maybe this won't be so bad!*

Katy's Mom nodded. "I think I have a can of tuna in the cabinet."

Great mom! I love tuna! And shrimp! Salem's spirits rose another notch. He would always love Sabrina and Hilda and Zelda the best, but Katy and her mom were okay.

And I'm not sneezing anymore!

"Come on, kitty." Katy shifted her hold so Salem's legs were dangling down.

Salem hated being carried that way! But he didn't dare struggle. If he upset Katy, her mom might not let him stay! Another new owner might not give him tuna.

Salem looked around when Katy carried him through the house. He spotted a chair that would make a perfect scratching post. And a small trash basket full of wadded-up papers to bat around. *So far so good!*

"What are you going to name him?" Katy's mom asked.

Katy put Salem on the kitchen floor. "Percy."

Percy! Salem blinked. *That's a terrible name for a cat! I hate the name Percy!*

But there was nothing Salem could do about it. He couldn't talk to mortals. So he couldn't tell them his real name.

"There you are, Percy." Katy's mom set a dish of tuna on the floor.

Yum! Salem dug right in. He finished eating all the tuna in less than a minute.

"Oh, my!" Katy's mom gasped. "If he's always that hungry, we'll have to feed him discount cat food!"

No! Salem shook his head. *I like King*

47

Kitty Gourmet! That's what the Spellmans always got me!

"I'm going to take Percy upstairs to my room now." Katy picked Salem up with his legs hanging down again.

Salem sighed. It *was* time for his morning nap. Things could be a lot worse, so he decided to put up with dangling legs. He just hoped Katy's bed was as comfortable as Sabrina's bed had been.

When Katy got upstairs, she turned into the bathroom. "Okay, Percy. It's time to get cleaned up."

I am clean! Salem huffed. *I gave myself forty licks just before I left home!*

Home. Salem sighed again. He missed the Spellmans already. But he couldn't go back. He'd have to get a shot every day!

Katy set Salem on the sink counter. Then she turned on the tap in the tub.

Salem was thinking about Sabrina and his toys. He wasn't paying attention. He was taken by surprise when Katy suddenly dropped him into the bathtub. It was full of water!

Oh, no! Salem scrambled to get out. He hated being all wet almost as much as he hated getting shots!

"Hold still, Percy!" Katy pushed Salem down. Then she dumped bubble bath into the water. "This will make you smell so good! Just like roses."

Talk about adding insult to injury! Salem was soaked and miserable. And now he was going to smell like a flower! No self-respecting cat would ever touch noses with him again.

Katy scrubbed Salem from his ears to

49

the tip of his tail. Then she took him out of the water and wrapped him in a big, fluffy towel.

Salem purred as Katy dried him off. She couldn't get all the water out of his fur, but the rubbing felt good. He relaxed when she carried him into her room. *Maybe now I can take my nap.*

Salem grinned when he saw Katy's bed. It was covered in a soft pink comforter. And it had lots of pillows. *Purr-fect!*

Katy put him on the floor, but Salem didn't get a chance to sleep. The little girl grabbed his tail when he tried to jump onto the bed.

Hey! Salem yelped. He decided not to argue, just curling up beside Katy on the rug.

Katy opened a wooden chest. "Now, let's see what you can wear. We're having a tea party today, Percy."

A tuxedo would be nice." Salem yawned. *I look great in a white shirt with a black tie.*

Salem opened one eye. Then both eyes. Katy was holding up a frilly white doll's dress and cap. *No way!*

But Salem didn't have a choice. If he wanted to live with Katy, he had to do what Katy wanted. And Katy wanted to play dress up the cat!

By that night, Salem was so tired he almost didn't care what Katy did.

He had been bathed, dressed, cuddled, and dangled all day.

He had sat on a tiny chair and lapped water out of a toy teacup for hours.

Then Katy had taken him for a walk in her doll carriage. That was so embarrassing!

And *then* her mom had fed him cheap dry cat food for dinner!

Now it was bedtime. Salem hid under Katy's bed when she came into the room.

"Where are you, Percy?" Katy looked under the bed. "We have to brush your teeth before we go to sleep."

Salem backed into the dark corner where Katy couldn't see him. The awful taste of discount cat food was still in his mouth.

But I'm not *going to let Katy brush my teeth!*

Salem didn't like living with Katy after all. She was a nice little girl, but she didn't know anything about cats!

Salem didn't know where the New Homes for Bad Cats people would send him. *But it has to be better than this!*

"Get me out of here!" Salem wailed.

Pop!

Salem blinked. He wasn't under Katy's bed anymore. He didn't know where he was.

But he was outside.

And it was very, very dark.

And really cold!

Chapter 6

"Where am I?" Salem woke up with a start. Then he remembered. He didn't want to stay with Katy. So the Bad Cats people had moved him to somewhere dark and cold.

Salem had crept into a barn that was full of other animals. Some of them were huge! But they didn't pay any attention to him.

He had slept on a pile of straw in a

small room. The grass wasn't as soft as Sabrina's bed. Still, it was warm and dry. And he had gone to sleep without brushing his teeth!

Salem shook bits of straw off his black fur. He sure didn't smell like roses anymore! But he was hungry and it was still dark outside. "Creepy."

A door creaked.

"Very creepy!" Salem shrank back. He looked through a hole in the wall. An old man in a red shirt and blue overalls walked in and turned on the barn lights.

A farmer! Salem suddenly felt better. Farmers were people, and people fed cats!

Salem moved to the door and stopped when all the other animals suddenly woke up.

A rooster crowed and chickens squawked.

55

Cows mooed and a giant horse stamped its feet.

Baby pigs squealed and a mama pig grunted.

Outside a dog barked.

Uh-oh. Salem didn't like dogs. The Bad Cats people must have sent him here by mistake. He couldn't live with a dog!

"Woof! Woof!" A big dog with long golden fur ran into the barn.

"Hey, Brute!" The farmer scratched behind the dog's ears. "Can't play now, boy. I've got work to do. Why don't you go get breakfast?"

Breakfast! Salem's mouth watered. Last night he dreamed that King Kitty had just invented clam cereal!

Boy! Do I miss the midnight snacks Sabrina used to give me.

"Woof! The big dog ran toward the

barn door. Then he stopped and turned. "Ruff, ruff, ruff!"

Uh-oh! Salem yowled. Brute was running right for him! *I'm toast if he catches me!*

Salem jumped onto a shelf. The fur on his back stood straight up. His tail fluffed out. He hissed, showing his fangs. He clawed at the dog's nose and missed.

Salem hoped he looked mean! He didn't *feel* mean.

Brute jumped up and down and barked.

Go away! Go away! Salem was scared, even though the dog couldn't reach him.

"What's going on, Brute?" The farmer ran in.

Saved! Salem stopped hissing.

"Well, hey, there!" The old man grinned when he saw Salem. He pushed the dog away. "Where'd you come from, little guy?"

Little guy? Salem didn't like that name, either. But it was better than Percy! He purred when the farmer petted his head. The man seemed really glad to see him, too!

Salem thought about that. Maybe the New Homes for Bad Cats people hadn't made a mistake. Katy had wanted a cat for her birthday. Maybe the farmer needed a cat, too.

And maybe the farmer doesn't let Brute into the house. Works for me!

"Bet you're hungry, huh, cat?" The man smiled. "Want some milk?"

I thought you'd never ask! But I'm not getting down until the dog is gone! Salem crouched and stared at Brute.

The farmer seemed to understand.

He took Brute outside and closed the barn door. "Okay! It's safe to come out now."

Salem leaped off the shelf and ran out of the room. The farmer was standing by the cows. Salem sat down and waited.

"Get ready, cat," the farmer said.

I'm ready! I'm ready!

Salem expected the farmer to pour him a saucer of milk like the Spellmans did. From a bottle they kept in the refrigerator. He didn't expect to be *squirted* with it!

Right from the cow! Yuck!

Salem sputtered as milk splashed all over his face. It stuck to his fur and whiskers. He licked it off. It was warm, but it tasted good!

"Want some more?" the farmer asked. "Open wide!"

Salem opened his mouth. Being squirted

59

with milk was disgusting, but he was too hungry to care.

The farmer stopped before Salem was full. "That's enough. I don't want to spoil your appetite."

That's the best news I've heard today. Salem sagged with relief. The man was going to feed him something else! *He'll probably serve me tuna in the can!*

"Okay, little guy. Here's the deal." The farmer looked down at Salem. "You can stay. But you've got to work if you want to eat. Just like everyone else."

Work! Salem stared at the man. *Cats eat and take naps and shed on the couch! We don't work!*

"But you'll love your job, little guy!" The farmer laughed.

I doubt it, but I'm listening. Salem

sighed. He had never worked before. He was sure he wouldn't like it.

"This barn is full of mice," the farmer said. "Your job is to catch them."

Catch mice! Salem's ears perked forward. He had to *chase* mice to catch mice. And chasing mice was one of his favorite things to do! That was more fun than chasing birds. *Wahoo!*

"Between the mice you catch and your morning milk, you won't starve." The old man nodded.

Salem gasped. The farmer wanted him to catch his own meals! He chased mice in the Spellmans' attic all the time. But he almost never caught one! And he had *never* eaten one!

I'm gonna starve!

"But don't go near the house, little guy. Brute doesn't like cats." The farmer started to milk his cows with loud machines.

Salem was very upset. He had been a first-class pet at the Spellmans. He had lived in a warm, dry house. They had fed him tuna and let him sleep on the beds.

Now I have to catch my own food and live in a barn! And take milk showers every morning! Salem sobbed. At least he didn't have to get shots or let Katy brush his teeth. He decided to get to work.

Salem had no trouble finding mice. He chased them all over the barn. It was fun at first, but not for long.

The mice knew where to hide. They got away through small holes where Salem couldn't follow. They hid in small places where Salem couldn't reach. They were faster than the mice in the Spellmans attic, too.

Salem didn't even take a nap! He chased mice all day, but he didn't catch one.

Until just before the sun went down.

The farmer was in the house, and the barn animals were quiet.

Salem crouched in a shadow by a mouse hole. He had given up chasing the mice. That didn't work.

I just have to stay very still. Salem stared at the hole. He didn't even twitch his tail. He hoped the mice didn't hear his stomach growling.

He was hungrier than ever now.

Finally a tiny brown mouse head looked out the hole.

Salem tensed, but he didn't move. He waited until the mouse came toward him. He had to time everything just right.

If I'm not too weak to pounce!

63

Salem waited until the mouse was very close. Then he leaped and slapped his paw down. "Dinner!"

The mouse wiggled under Salem's toes.

"I did it! I caught a mouse! All by myself!" Salem was so excited!

"Squeak!" the mouse cried.

"I didn't hear that." Salem stared at the trapped mouse. If he lifted his paw, it would get away. "Sorry, mouse, but I've got to eat something!"

"Squeak, squeak!" The mouse stared back at Salem. Then it blinked its little brown eyes.

"But I can't eat *someone!*" Salem lifted his paw.

The mouse dashed back into its hole.

"So I guess I'll have to starve!" Salem flopped on his stomach.

He didn't like living on a farm at all! He

wanted cold milk in a saucer. He wanted
a house without a dog. And mostly he
wanted food that didn't squeak!

There was only one thing to do.

"Hey! Bad Cats people! I'm ready to try
another new home!"

Salem sat up and held his breath.

Pop!

He was outside in the dark again. But it
wasn't quiet!

Metal cans crashed and clanged. A police
siren wailed. A lot of cats yowled nearby.

Something whizzed over Salem's head.
He dropped on his stomach. The ground
was cold, wet, and hard.

"Get out of here, cats!" a mean man
yelled.

A tin can hit the wall behind Salem and
fell. He shivered as the can rolled up to
his nose. *Uh-oh.*

Chapter 7

Salem was cold and scared.

He was also really insulted!

Being a kid's cat was embarrassing. Being a barnyard cat was too much work! But now the New Homes for Bad Cats people had turned him into an alley cat!

"I like to visit alleys," Salem moaned. "But I don't want to live in one!"

Salem stood up and licked his fur. It

was already damp and dirty. Staying in an alley was not going to work.

"Listen up, Bad Cats people. Let's just move on to home number four."

Salem took a deep breath and waited to pop.

Nothing happened!

"Hey!" Salem shouted. "Are you Bad Cats guys awake?"

"Scram, cats!" A man threw a tin can from a window high above. "And don't come back!"

Salem jumped aside. The tin can just missed him. It bounced and clattered on the paved alley.

"Okay, Bad Cats people. I'm ready whenever you are!" Salem looked up.

But nothing happened.

"Oh, no!" Salem suddenly remembered that he only had three new homes to try.

And the alley was number three!

"I'm a *stray!*"

Salem sobbed. Now he was hungry *and* cold. And there wasn't even a barn! No straw to curl up in. No cow's milk to drink. And no cute mice that he couldn't eat anyway.

"What am I going to do?"

Salem looked up and down the dark alley. No one answered. There weren't any people around.

"Well, I can talk to myself now."

Other cats yowled again. The local cat crowd was gathering for the night.

Salem decided to find them. Alley cats knew where to find food. They knew all the warm, dry places to sleep. He was stuck in the alley now. So he had to make friends with the other stray cats.

"If I want to eat and take naps."

Salem trotted down the alley. He could see the other cats on top of a fence under a streetlight.

At least I won't be alone. And alley cats don't get shots!

"Hey!" Salem called out when he reached the end of the alley. He counted eight cats on the fence.

A yellow tabby looked down and blinked. The other cats ignored him.

"I was just passing by," Salem said. The other cats couldn't talk and didn't understand him. But talking made him feel better. "Where's a good place to grab a snack around here?"

A big, gray cat with yellow eyes jumped down. It stared at Salem for a minute, then hissed a warning.

"I was just asking!" Salem fluffed his tail. He didn't want to look scared. The other cats were watching. He tried talking like the cats in his old neighborhood. "Yeow, meow."

The gray cat swung at Salem with its claws!

"What'd I say?" Salem jumped back. "Where I come from, that means, 'What's up, guys?' "

The gray cat didn't understand. Or it didn't want to be friendly. It hissed and growled.

Salem nodded. "Okay. You're the boss."

The gray cat turned and left through a hole in the fence. The other cats jumped down on the far side.

Salem was alone again.

"But not for long." Salem went through the hole, too. He was still really hungry. He hoped the other cats were looking for food.

Salem followed the band of strays, but he stayed far behind. It would take time to make friends. He'd just watch and wait. *Until I learn the alley cat rules.*

The stray cats darted around a building. Salem stopped at the corner to watch what they did.

The strays crept along the back of the building. They all stopped when a man came out a door.

A delicious odor tickled Salem's nose! *Pizza!*

The man put a bag in a trash can and went back inside.

When the man was gone, the other cats moved again. They began digging through the trash cans. And they were very quiet.

"Wahoo! Food!" Salem shouted and ran forward. He was so hungry, he forgot that he didn't know the alley cat rules. He leaped into the nearest trash can. And it fell over!

"Oops!"

The metal can clanked and rolled with Salem inside.

The surprised strays yowled.

The man ran back outside with a broom! "Shoo! Go away! Get out of here, cats!"

Salem peeked out of the can. He dropped a pizza crust when he gasped. The man was chasing the other cats away!

"You, too!" The man kicked Salem's trash can hard.

I'm gone! Salem bolted into the alley. He didn't even take time to grab his pizza. He ran as fast as he could after the other cats.

The strays were waiting for him by the alley fence.

"Sorry about that." Salem stopped a few feet away. "I'm new here. I'll get the hang of alley cat life soon. I promise."

The gray cat crouched and moved toward him.

"Rule number one." Salem backed up a step. "No shouting at feeding time."

The other cats moved toward Salem, too. They all looked really mad!

Uh-oh.

"Come on, guys!" Salem pleaded. "How about a second chance?"

The gray cat sprang toward him, hissing and spitting.

Salem turned and ran away.

The gray cat chased Salem down the street! When it gave up and left, Salem ducked into a big pipe.

73

"Now what am I going to do?" Salem was so miserable. It wasn't *just* because he was sitting in a puddle in a pipe. Or that he was starving. Or that he was all alone.

Salem didn't really care about those things.

He missed Sabrina and Hilda and Zelda. Home with the Spellmans was better than anywhere else.

"Even if I have to eat discount cat food," Salem sobbed. "And brush my teeth. And sleep on straw. And get a shot every day *forever!*"

But Salem couldn't go back to his old house and family. He had decided to live somewhere else because he didn't want an allergy shot every day.

And he had used up his three chances.

It was too late.

"I want to go home!" Salem sobbed.

Chapter 8

Salem flopped on his stomach in the pipe and closed his eyes. His fur got wet in the puddle, but he didn't care.

"I wouldn't mind smelling like roses if I could just go home!" Salem cried. "I'd even work to catch the mice in the attic!"

He missed Sabrina and her aunts *so* much!

Pop!

"And I wouldn't care if I had to get *two* allergy shots every day!" Salem sobbed. He still had his eyes closed.

"You'll only need *one* shot a day," Hilda said.

Salem sighed sadly. Now he was *imagining* things. He could hear Hilda's voice.

He kept his eyes shut and pretended he was home on the kitchen counter.

Zelda chuckled. "I think he missed us."

Now I'm hearing Zelda, too! Salem sneezed. "Achoo!"

"Salem!" Sabrina exclaimed. "You're back!"

"I am?" Salem's eyes popped open. He *was* lying on the kitchen counter at home. Hilda, Zelda, and Sabrina were all smiling at him! "This isn't a dream, is it?"

"Nope." Sabrina patted Salem's head. "You're home."

"But how?" Salem sat up. His wet fur dripped on the counter. He sneezed twice. "I used up my three chances."

"You had three chances to try *new* homes." Zelda picked up Salem's dish.

"And then you found out that you really wanted to live at your *real* home," Hilda said. "No matter what."

Sabrina nodded. "So the Bad Cats people gave you a second chance and sent you back here."

"I'm so glad to see you!" Salem leaped into Sabrina's arms. He rubbed against her face and purred. "I never want to leave home again. Achoo!"

"Good." Sabrina grinned. "Because we really missed you, too."

77

"Would you like tuna or salmon for dinner, Salem?" Zelda asked.

"I'll eat anything!" Salem jumped back to the counter. He decided not to mention discount cat food. "Achoo! Achoo! Achoo!"

"You can eat later, Salem." Hilda sighed. "First you have to get your allergy shot."

Salem blinked, but he didn't argue. If he wanted to stay home, he had to take his shots. "Okay. But can't we go to the vet's after dinner? I'm so hungry."

"We aren't going to the vet's." Hilda pointed. A huge shot needle appeared in her hand.

Salem gasped. "What's that? Achoo!"

"You have an Other Realm allergy, Salem." Zelda spooned tuna into his bowl.

Hilda shrugged. "So I get to give you your shot!"

Salem didn't like that at all! Hilda

wasn't a vet! But he didn't complain. His eyes were watering and his skin started to itch.

"Achoo! Achoo! Then let's get it over with."

"Just close your eyes, Salem," Sabrina said.

Salem closed his eyes. He held his breath. He felt a sting. "Ow!"

"All done." Hilda pointed and the shot needle disappeared. "Now, that wasn't so bad, was it?"

"It was totally awful. But now I don't have to worry about getting another one." Salem shuddered. "Until tomorrow."

Zelda put Salem's dish on the counter. He pounced on the bowl and started to eat.

"You won't be getting a shot tomorrow," Hilda said.

Salem snapped his head up. "Why not?"

"Because this time you had a one-shot allergy, Salem." Zelda folded her arms. She looked very serious. "*Next* time it will take a lot more than one shot to cure you."

"Hey, Salem!" Sabrina grinned. "You're not sneezing anymore!"

Salem sat back. He wasn't sneezing! His eyes and skin felt fine, too! "I'm cured! And no more shots!"

"Not until next week," Hilda said. "You have another appointment at the vet's for your regular cat shots."

"And we expect you to go and behave!" Zelda added.

"I will." Salem nodded. At least, regular cats only got shots once a year. "Cat's honor."

"Thanks, Salem." Sabrina gave him a hug. "It just wasn't the same around here without you."

"I really missed you, too." Salem purred. Then he huffed. "But I still *hate* getting shots!"

Cat Care Tips

1. All cats should see their veterinarian at least once a year for a full checkup and vaccines. Older cats (older than eleven years) should see their veterinarian twice a year for checkups.
2. You should take your cat to the veterinarian if you notice any of the following:
   a) your cat has not eaten anything in twenty-four hours.
   b) your cat has not eaten as much as usual in the last two to three days.
   c) your cat is drinking more water than he or she usually does.
   d) your cat seems to be getting skinny.
   e) your cat is going to the litter box more often than normal or is crying when he or she goes to the box.
   f) your cat's coat is not as shiny as it used to be.
   g) your cat is hiding or does not want to play like he or she usually does.

h) your cat is not keeping himself or herself clean.
i) your cat has not had a bowel movement in two days.

—Laura E. Smiley, MS, DVM, Dipl. ACVIM
Gwynedd Veterinary Hospital

EASY TO READ-
FUN TO SOLVE!

THE
NANCY DREW
NOTEBOOKS®

**JOIN NANCY AND HER BEST FRIENDS
AS THEY COLLECT CLUES
AND SOLVE MYSTERIES
IN THE NANCY DREW NOTEBOOKS®
STARTING WITH**

#1 THE SLUMBER PARTY SECRET

#2 THE LOST LOCKET

#3 THE SECRET SANTA

#4 BAD DAY FOR BALLET

Look for a brand-new story every
other month wherever books are sold

EASY TO READ—FUN TO SOLVE!

**Meet up with suspense and mystery
in The Hardy Boys® are:**

THE CLUES™
BROTHERS

Available from Minstrel® Books
Published by Pocket Books

2389